Amelia Bedelia's Family Album

by **PEGGY PARISH**

pictures by **LYNN SWEAT**

SCHOLASTIC INC.
New York Toronto London Auckland Sydney
Mexico City New Delhi Hong Kong

ISBN 0-439-13301-7

Published by Scholastic Inc., 555 Broadway, New York, NY 10012, by arrangement with Greenwillow Books.
SCHOLASTIC and associated logos are trademarks and/or registered trademarks of Scholastic Inc.

12 11 10 9 8 7 6 5 4 3 2 1   9/9 0 1 2 3 4/0

Printed in the U.S.A.   23

First Scholastic printing, March 1999

FOR
SUSAN HIRSCHMAN,
WHO'S BEEN WITH ME
ALL THE WAY,
WITH LOVE

"Amelia Bedelia," said Mrs. Rogers,
"you have been here a long time."
"Oh, Mrs. Rogers," said Amelia Bedelia,
"are you tired of me?"
"Of course not," said Mrs. Rogers.

"We want to have a party for you.
We want to meet your family."
"Now that is nice," said Amelia Bedelia.
"Who would you like to invite?"
asked Mrs. Rogers.

"I'll get my family album,"
said Amelia Bedelia.
"You can help me decide."
"Good idea," said Mr. Rogers.
Amelia Bedelia got her album.

"This is my daddy,"
said Amelia Bedelia.
"He is a telephone operator."

"Then he helps people make calls,"
said Mr. Rogers.

"He does not!" said Amelia Bedelia.
"He operates on telephones."
"I see," said Mr. Rogers.

"This is my mama," said Amelia Bedelia. "She is a loafer."

"You mean she does nothing," said Mrs. Rogers.

"Certainly not," said Amelia Bedelia.
"She works hard. She makes
dough into loaves of bread.
That's what a loafer does."
"I see," said Mrs. Rogers.

"This is Uncle Albert,"
said Amelia Bedelia.
"He is a big-game hunter."
"You mean
he kills animals?"
asked Mrs. Rogers.

"Why would he do that!"
said Amelia Bedelia.
"He hunts big games.
He has one so big
it takes up a whole room."
"I see," said Mrs. Rogers.

"Next is Aunt Mary," said Amelia Bedelia. "She is a bank teller."

"Then she cashes people's checks," said Mr. Rogers.

"No," said Amelia Bedelia,
"she tells everybody
in the bank
where to go.
Some folks don't like that."
"I see," said Mr. Rogers.

"This is Cousin Calvin," said Amelia Bedelia. "He is a boxer."

"Does he win any matches?" asked Mrs. Rogers.

Amelia Bedelia looked puzzled.
"Matches!" she said.
"Why would he win matches?
A boxer packs boxes.
He gets paid money."
"I see," said Mrs. Rogers.

"Cousin Edward
is a horse
racer," said
Amelia Bedelia.
"Oh, he is
a jockey,"
said Mr. Rogers.

"I don't think so," said Amelia Bedelia.
"Cousin Edward races horses.
He almost won once.
But he tripped and fell."
"I see," said Mr. Rogers.

"Uncle Ned is a Cook,"
said Amelia Bedelia.
"He works in a hotel."
"Then he is a chef,"
said Mrs. Rogers.

"No," said Amelia Bedelia.
"He is a doorman.
His name is Ned Cook."
"I see," said Mrs. Rogers.

"Uncle Dan takes pictures,"
said Amelia Bedelia.
"What kind of pictures
does he take?" asked Mr. Rogers.

"Any kind," said Amelia Bedelia.
"You really have to watch him.
He will take every picture
in the house."
"I see," said Mr. Rogers.

"Cousin Bea
has a fun job,"
said Amelia
Bedelia.
"She balances
checkbooks."

"I wish
she would
balance mine,"
said Mrs. Rogers.

"She will," said Amelia Bedelia.
"She can balance twenty at one time."
"I see," said Mrs. Rogers.

"My brother Ike
wants an orange grove,"
said Amelia Bedelia,
"but he has bad luck."
"How is that?"
asked Mr. Rogers.

"He orders orange trees,"
said Amelia Bedelia,
"but they all come out green."
"I see," said Mr. Rogers.

"This is poor Cousin Chester,"
said Amelia Bedelia.
"He is a printer."
"What does he print?"
asked Mrs. Rogers.

"Everything," said Amelia Bedelia.
"We could never teach him
proper writing."
"I see," said Mrs. Rogers.

"Cousin Clara is a bookkeeper,"
said Amelia Bedelia.
"She must be good with numbers,"
said Mr. Rogers.

"No," said Amelia Bedelia.
"But she is good at keeping books.
She never returns one."
"I see," said Mr. Rogers.

"Cousin Ella
works with Clay,"
said Amelia
Bedelia.

"Is she a potter?" asked Mrs. Rogers.
"I don't know any Potters,"
said Amelia Bedelia.

"Ella and her husband Clay
have a bakery."
"I see," said Mrs. Rogers.

"Uncle Alf is a garbage collector,"
said Amelia Bedelia.
"That is smelly work,"
said Mr. Rogers.

"It sure is," said Amelia Bedelia.
"All of his neighbors moved away."
"I see," said Mr. Rogers.

"Cousin Susan belongs to a
fan club." said Amelia Bedelia.
"Are there many fans in her club?"
asked Mr. Rogers.

"Oh yes," said Amelia Bedelia.
"You never saw so many
different kinds of fans."
"I see," said Mr. Rogers.

"My niece Lulu stuffs olives,"
said Amelia Bedelia.
"Does she stuff the pimento
in the middle?"
asked Mrs. Rogers.

"No," said Amelia Bedelia,
"she stuffs olives into herself."
"I see," said Mrs. Rogers.

"The last picture
is of Ollie,"
said Amelia Bedelia,
"He is my nephew.
Ollie is our catcher."

"What does he catch?" asked Mr. Rogers.

"Everything," said Amelia Bedelia.
"Measles, mumps, colds.
Whatever comes along,
Ollie catches it."

"What an unusual family,"
said Mrs. Rogers.
"Yes," said Mr. Rogers.
"Invite all of them to the party."

"All right," said Amelia Bedelia.
She left the room.

In a bit she came back.
"They will be here tomorrow,"
she said.

"Tomorrow!" said Mrs. Rogers.
"We can't get everything ready by then."

"What's to get ready?"
asked Amelia Bedelia.
"Food!" said Mr. Rogers.
"Now, Mr. Rogers," said Amelia Bedelia,
"my folks know about parties.
They will bring the food."

"But Amelia Bedelia," said Mrs. Rogers,
"will there be enough food for everybody?"
"Everybody!" said Amelia Bedelia.
"I hadn't thought of inviting everybody.
What a good idea!"

She ran outside.

"Hear! Hear!" she shouted.

"A party tomorrow.

Everybody come."

And everybody came!